THE CHILD'S WORLD®

The Tale of Peter Rabbit

Written by Beatrix Potter • Illustrated by Wendy Rasmussen

The Child's World

For Timothy and Grace

Published in the United States of America by The Child's World®
1980 Lookout Drive • Mankato, MN 56003-1705
800-599-READ • www.childsworld.com

ACKNOWLEDGMENTS
The Child's World®: Mary Berendes, Publishing Director
Editorial Directions, Inc.: E. Russell Primm, Editor; Dina Rubin, Proofreader
The Design Lab: Kathleen Petelinsek, Design; Victoria Stanley, Production Assistant

TEXT

ILLUSTRATIONS

LIBRARY OF CONGRESS CATALOGING-IN-PUBLICATION DATA
Potter, Beatrix, 1866–1943.
  The tale of Peter Rabbit / by Beatrix Potter ; illustrated by Wendy Rasmussen.
    p. cm. — (Classic tales)
  Summary: Peter disobeys his mother by going into Mr. McGregor's garden and almost gets caught.
  ISBN 978-1-60253-295-3 (library bound : alk. paper)
  [1. Rabbits—Fiction.] I. Rasmussen, Wendy, 1952– ill. II. Title. III. Series.
  PZ7.P85Tap 2009
  [E]—dc22   2009001636

The Tale of Peter Rabbit

nce upon a time, there were four little rabbits, and their names were Flopsy, Mopsy, Cotton-tail, and Peter.

They lived with their mother in a sandbank, underneath the root of a very big fir tree.

"Now, my dears," said old Mrs.
Rabbit one morning, "you may go into
the fields or down the lane, but don't go
into Mr. McGregor's garden.

"Your father had an accident there. He was put in a pie by Mrs. McGregor."

"Now run along and don't get into mischief. I am going out."

Then old Mrs. Rabbit took a basket and her umbrella and went through the wood to the baker's.

She bought a loaf of brown bread and five currant buns.

Flopsy, Mopsy, and Cotton-tail, who were good little bunnies, went down the lane together to gather blackberries.

But Peter, who was very naughty, ran straight away to Mr. McGregor's garden and squeezed under the gate!

First he ate some lettuces and some French beans.

And then he ate some radishes.

And then, feeling rather sick, he went to look for some parsley.

But around the end of a cucumber frame, whom should he meet but Mr. McGregor!

Mr. McGregor was on his hands and knees planting out young cabbages, but he jumped up and ran after Peter, waving a rake and calling out, "Stop thief!"

Peter was most dreadfully frightened. He rushed all over the garden, for he had forgotten the way back to the gate.

He lost one shoe among the cabbages
and the other among the potatoes.

After losing them, he ran on four legs
and went faster.

So that I think he might have got away altogether if he had not unfortunately run into a gooseberry net and got caught by the large buttons on his jacket.

It was a blue jacket with brass buttons, quite new.

Peter gave himself up for lost
and shed big tears, but his sobs were
overheard by some friendly sparrows
who flew to him in great excitement and
begged him to exert himself.

Mr. McGregor came up with a sieve,
which he intended to pop on the top of
Peter, but Peter wriggled out just in time.

Leaving his jacket behind him.

He rushed into the toolshed and
jumped into a can.

It would have been a beautiful thing
to hide in, if it had not had so much
water in it. Mr. McGregor was quite
sure that Peter was somewhere in the

toolshed, perhaps hidden underneath
a flowerpot.

He began to turn them over carefully,
looking under each.

Presently, Peter sneezed, "*Kertyschoo!*"

Mr. McGregor was after him in no time and tried to put his foot upon Peter, who jumped out of a window, upsetting three plants.

Peter sat down to rest. He was out of breath and trembling with fright, and he had not the least idea which way to go.

Also, he was very damp with sitting in that can.

After a time, he began to wander about, going

lippity—

lippity—

not very fast and looking all around.

He found a door in a wall, but it was locked and there was no room for a fat little rabbit to squeeze underneath.

An old mouse was running in and out over the stone doorstep, carrying peas and beans to her family in the wood. Peter asked her the way to the gate, but she had such a large pea in her mouth she could not answer. She only shook her head at him.

Peter began to cry.

Then he tried to find his way straight across the garden, but he became more and more puzzled. Presently, he came to a pond where Mr. McGregor filled

his water cans. A white cat was staring at
some goldfish. She sat very, very still, but
now and then the tip of her tail twitched
as if it were alive. Peter thought it best to
go away without speaking to her.

He had heard about cats from his
cousin, little Benjamin Bunny.

He went back toward the toolshed,
but suddenly, quite close to him, he heard
the noise of a hoe—*scr-r-ritch, scratch,
scratch, scritch.*

Peter ran underneath the bushes, but
presently as nothing happened, he came
out and climbed upon a wheelbarrow,
and peeped over.

The first thing he saw was Mr. McGregor hoeing onions. His back was turned toward Peter, and beyond him was the gate!

Peter got down very quietly off the
wheelbarrow and started running as fast
as he could go, along a straight walk
behind some black currant bushes.

Mr. McGregor caught sight of him at the corner, but Peter did not care. He slipped underneath the gate and was safe at last in the wood outside the garden.

Mr. McGregor hung up the little jacket and the shoes for a scarecrow to frighten the blackbirds.

Peter never stopped running or looked behind him till he got home to the big fir tree.

He was so tired that he flopped down upon the nice soft sand on the floor of the rabbit hole and shut his eyes. His mother was busy cooking. She wondered what he had done with his clothes.

It was the second little jacket and pair of shoes that Peter had lost in two weeks!

I am sorry to say that Peter was not very well during the evening. His mother put him to bed and made some chamomile tea, and she gave a dose of it to Peter! "One teaspoonful to be taken at bedtime." But—

Flopsy, Mopsy, and Cotton-tail had bread and milk and blackberries for supper.

ABOUT BEATRIX POTTER

When Beatrix Potter (1866–1943) was growing up in England, she did not go to a regular school. Instead, she stayed at home and was educated by a governess. Beatrix didn't have many playmates, other than her brother, but she had numerous pets, including birds, mice, lizards, and snakes. She enjoyed drawing her pets, and they later served as inspiration for her books.

As a young girl, Beatrix enjoyed going for walks in the country. She began drawing the animals and plants she saw. For several years, she also kept a secret journal, written in her own special code. The journal's code was not understood until after Beatrix died.

In 1893, when Potter was twenty-seven years old, she wrote a story for a little boy who was sick. That story became *The Tale of Peter Rabbit*. In 1902, the book was published and featured illustrations drawn by Potter herself. Her next book was *The Tale of Squirrel Nutkin*, which was published in 1903. Potter went on to write twenty-three books, all that were easy for children to read.

When Potter was in her forties, she bought a place called Hill Top Farm in England. She began breeding sheep and became a respected farmer. She was concerned about the farmland and preserving natural places. When she died, Potter left all of her property, about 4,000 acres (1,600 hectares), to England's National Trust. This land is now part of the Lake District National Park. Today, the National Trust manages the Beatrix Potter Gallery, which displays her original book illustrations.

ABOUT WENDY RASMUSSEN

Drawing from the time she could hold her first crayon, Wendy Rasmussen grew up on a farm in southern New Jersey surrounded by the animals and things that often appear in her work. Rasmussen studied both biology and art in college. Today she illustrates children's books, as well as medical and natural-science books.

Today, Rasmussen lives in Bucks County, Pennsylvania, with her black Labrador Caley and her cat Josephine. When not in her studio, Rasmussen can usually be found somewhere in the garden or kayaking on the Delaware River.

OTHER WORKS BY BEATRIX POTTER

The Tale of Peter Rabbit (1902)

The Tale of Squirrel Nutkin (1903)

The Tailor of Gloucester (1903)

The Tale of Benjamin Bunny (1904)

The Tale of Two Bad Mice (1904)

The Tale of Mrs. Tiggy-Winkle (1905)

The Tale of the Pie and the Patty-Pan (1905)

The Tale of Mr. Jeremy Fisher (1906)

The Story of a Fierce Bad Rabbit (1906)

The Story of Miss Moppet (1906)

The Tale of Tom Kitten (1907)

The Tale of Jemima Puddle-Duck (1908)

The Tale of Samuel Whiskers or, The Roly-Poly Pudding (1908)

The Tale of the Flopsy Bunnies (1909)

The Tale of Ginger and Pickles (1909)

The Tale of Mrs. Tittlemouse (1910)

The Tale of Timmy Tiptoes (1911)

The Tale of Mr. Tod (1912)

The Tale of Pigling Bland (1913)

Appley Dapply's Nursery Rhymes (1917)

The Tale of Johnny Town-Mouse (1918)